"When everyone clapped for Ben, I was annoyed. That applause was supposed to be mine. Not some sixth grader's. Not my half brother's."

CARTER RAMOS

Age: 13
Hometown: Dallas, TX

STONE ARCH BOOKS
presents

TONY HAWK

LIVE 2 SKATE

RIVAL

written by
BLAKE A. HOENA

images by
FERNANDO CANO AND JOE AZPEYTIA

a
CAPSTONE
production

Published by Stone Arch Books
A Capstone Imprint
1710 Roe Crest Drive, North Mankato, Minnesota 56003
www.capstonepub.com

Printed in Canada.
092013   007763FRSNS14

Library of Congress Cataloging-in-Publication Data is
available on the Library of Congress website.
Hardcover: 978-1-4342-3847-4
Paperback: 978-1-4342-6562-3

Summary: Carter and his younger half-brother Ben compete
for a star spot on the skate team.

Designer: Bob Lentz
Creative Director: Heather Kindseth

Design Elements: Shutterstock.

CHAPTERS

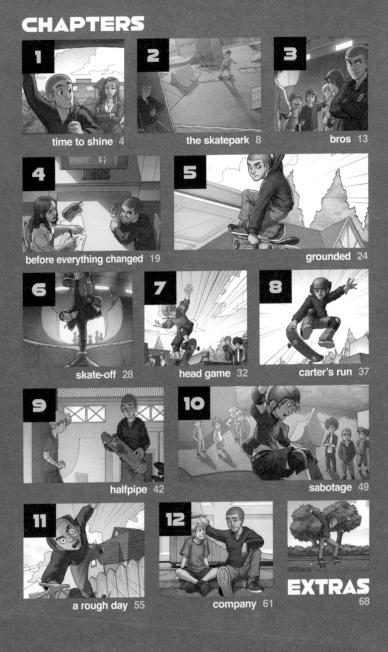

TIME TO SHINE

It was just the second week of school, but Carter Ramos already knew that this was going to be his year. He could feel it. As an eighth grader, he was one of the oldest kids at Ben Franklin Middle School. He was also going to be one of the veterans of the junior skateboarding club. That meant no more standing in the shadows of older kids. No more fighting for his chance to skate. Now was his time to shine.

Sure, the team had other good skaters. Chatty could hit the halfpipes pretty hard, while Sprig was solid on the street course. They were eighth graders, too, but Carter felt he had the edge on his friends. He could carve it up and grind it out no matter the venue.

Yeah, this was going to be his year. At least that's what Carter was thinking as he stood out in the school parking lot. He leaned against his mother's little blue Honda while he was waiting for her to finish up with her last class. His mom worked as the school's Spanish interpreter. Mostly she helped Latino parents keep track of what was going on with their kids. But during the last couple hours of the day, she tutored students who needed help with their English.

Carter saw his mom's head of thick brown hair poke out the back door. She waved, so he waved back. As she walked over, his mother hit the car's remote lock and the trunk popped open. She kept his board, helmet, and pads in her car during the day. That way, as his mother liked to say, he wouldn't be tempted to mess around at school. There were "No Skateboarding" signs posted all over the grounds. Her rule: if he stayed out of trouble, she let him hit the local skatepark while she met with parents after school. If he didn't stay out of trouble, he had a long bus ride home.

Today was the skateboarding club's first meeting, when all the ground rules would be spelled out. Carter was excited to get going. He couldn't wait to show off a little for the new

crop of sixth graders, as well as remind the seventh graders that he and his friends were now king.

The club met at the local skatepark. Chatty and Sprig were probably already there. They didn't have to wait on their mothers, so they headed over straight after school. Carter hastily grabbed his deck from the trunk and slung his backpack full of pads over his shoulder. His helmet was strapped to the outside of his pack. He was about to run off when his mother called him back.

"What, no, 'Hello'? No, 'Good-bye'?" she chided him. "No, 'I love you, Momma. Thanks for bringing my skateboard to school for me'?"

Looking around to make sure none of his friends were near, Carter ran up to his mom. He gave her a quick peck on the cheek.

"*Gracias*, Momma," was all he said.

She playfully tousled his hair and winked.

Then he was off.

"No skateboarding in the parking lot!" she yelled after him.

THE SKATEPARK

Once he stepped onto the sidewalk that bordered the school, he laid his board down. Hopping on, he pushed himself forward. The skatepark was only a mile or so from school.

Carter listened to the hum of his wheels on the pavement. He found it comforting as he watched houses whiz by. Some skaters plugged into their MP3s as soon as they jumped onto their boards. Not Carter. He liked the sound of his wheels carving back and forth against concrete or wood. The hum helped him feel connected to his board, helped him know what it was doing underneath him.

Up ahead was a large crack in the sidewalk. As Carter neared it, he pushed back on the tail of his board with his left foot and ollied over it. The trick was just a warm-up to see how things were feeling today. Along the way, he found other obstacles. Sometimes he'd do a kickflip as he skated off a curb to cross a street. Other times he'd ollie 180 in the middle of the sidewalk to avoid some crumbling pavement.

Since no one was watching, he thought he'd be a little daring. As he skated up to a kid's toy doll left in the middle of the sidewalk, he popped his board up for an ollie, but then with his back foot, he spun the board for a 360 pop shuvit. When he went to land the trick, his front foot missed the deck and slapped down on the sidewalk. His momentum caused him to roll forward into someone's yard.

Carter quickly got up and grabbed his board. Brushing himself off as he ran, he darted down the block before he jumped back on. He hoped none of his friends were around to see or they'd razz him a bit for taking a spill. He could hit a 180 pop shuvit any day, but the 360 was a bit tougher.

Carter was surprised when he reached the skatepark. Hardly anyone was outside on the street course, except for

some newbs. They wobbled and tumbled as they attempted ollies and grinds. Carter glanced at his watch. It was still a little early, so where was everyone? It was a gorgeous day out. He had thought more skaters would be on the street course.

There were two parts to the skatepark. One was a fenced in slab of concrete for the street course. There were the typical spines and rails, launch boxes and banks. But it didn't stop there. There was even a drop-in at one end and a mini halfpipe at the other.

The other part of the skatepark was indoors, where the halfpipes were. There were two of them: a small five footer and a twelve footer. Kids at the skatepark liked to call them Little Vert and Big Vert. Carter picked up his board at the doorway as he headed in.

It was dark inside. He could barely see, but he could hear the familiar hum of his wheels carving against wood. The sound brought a smile to his face.

Something exciting must be going on, he thought. He could see a bunch of shadowy shapes gathered next to Big Vert. Whoever was on it was skating hard. Carter could tell by the hard click of wheels against the copings as the skater shot up the sides of the verts.

He joined the crowd and saw his crew, Chatty and Sprig. Chatty was a Chinese kid whose real name was Hai Tan. He immediately started talking when he saw Carter. That's actually how Chatty had gotten his nickname. He couldn't keep quiet, especially when he was excited about something.

". . . I've never seen him, but he did this Muska frontside flip and then . . ." Chatty rambled, ". . . and then he busted out a frontside 360 grab . . ."

Carter let the words flow in one ear and out the other. He wanted to get a good look at this skater who could be his competition on the skate club. Carter squeezed his way forward. The kid on Big Vert was smallish — maybe a new sixth grader. Carter hadn't met many of the sixth graders at school. He only knew the ones who hit the skatepark over the summer. But he was pretty sure he had never seen this kid here — or at school — before.

Then, as his eyes adjusted to the dim lights inside, he was stunned to realize who was on Big Vert.

"I know him," Carter said.

"What do you mean, you know him?" Chatty asked.

"Yeah, who is he?" Sprig asked.

Sprig was his other best bud. His real name was Dewain Cook. He had earned his nickname a couple years ago. One spring, he was just a stubby little kid, but during the summer, he shot up, tall and thin. His dad had said he looked like a "sprig" of parsley with his bushy Afro. So from then on, he'd been known as Sprig.

"Come on, tell us," Chatty pleaded.

"That's my little brother, Ben," Carter said.

His friends' jaws dropped.

"That white kid?" Sprig said.

"My dad had Ben shortly after he divorced my mom," Carter replied.

"I knew you had a brother," Chatty said, "but I didn't know he could skate."

"Or that he was white," Sprig added.

"Dude, my dad's white," Carter shot back.

Carter didn't know Ben could skate either, at least not like this. When they were younger, Carter used to visit Ben and their dad on weekends. He'd show Ben the new tricks that he'd learned. Then Ben would try to copy him, which usually meant Ben would fall and scrape a knee. The last time he had hung out with his brother was a few years ago. Back then, Ben could barely ollie.

Ben was greeted with a round of applause when he finished. The sound grated on Carter, made him seethe inside. That applause was supposed to be his. After all, this was his year. Not some sixth grader's. Not his half brother's.

When Ben climbed down from the deck, a few of the other young skaters gathered around to congratulate him on a good run. Carter hung back with his friends, the eighth graders. He saw Ben's eyes light up when he looked

Carter's way, but all Carter did was give him a slight nod of recognition.

This being the club's first meeting, there was no skating going on once Rubin started talking. Rubin ran the skatepark and sponsored its junior club for kids in middle school.

"We'll have official practices every Monday and Thursday," Rubin explained. "But you can use the skatepark whenever it's open."

Rubin went on to say that competitions would be held every other weekend. At home events, everyone would get a chance to skate. When the club traveled, the top three street skaters and the top three halfpipe skaters would represent the club. Those top skaters would be decided at a skate-off held the Thursday before an event. And if someone was considered one of the best in both street and halfpipe, then the skater got to compete in both events.

After he laid down the rules, Rubin added, "Everyone is free to stick around and practice on their own today. We've been invited to compete against a club across town next Saturday. So that means our first skate-off will be next Thursday. Be prepared to skate for keeps."

Last year Carter had made it to about half of the traveling events. Sprig and Chatty had also made it to a couple, but usually it was the older kids — eighth graders — competing. That meant that this year, it would be him and his friends dominating things.

Carter looked around the group. There were three eighth graders, five seventh graders, and five sixth graders, including his half brother.

"Looks like we should be should be hitting all the traveling events together," Sprig said.

"Yeah, the *tres a-mee-goos*," Chatty said.

"Dude, we really need to work on that accent of yours," Carter shot back.

As they were talking, Ben strolled up to them. He looked out of place next to the older kids. He was much shorter than Carter and his friends, and scrawnier, too. His Vans were scuffed up and his jeans frayed at the cuffs. His Birdhouse T hung loose on him — probably a hand-me-down from their step-brother, his dad's wife's oldest son.

"Hey, bro," Ben said, "are you going to stick around and work the halfpipe tonight?"

"Bro?" Carter said putting his arms around Sprig and Chatty's shoulders. "These are my bros. These are the guys I'll be skating with while you and the other sixth graders are watching cartoons next Saturday."

With that, Carter turned and walked away. His friends came with him.

"Ouch, that was harsh, bro," Sprig said.

"Don't you know?" Chatty said. "Carter doesn't get along with his dad."

At least not since he got married, Carter thought. *Since he stopped coming to my Little League games and birthdays.*

"When's the last time you saw your little brother?" Sprig asked.

"Not sure," Carter replied. "It doesn't matter."

That night at home, Carter heard Ben's story — why he was joining the skate club.

"*Lo siento*," his mom began, apologizing because she had forgotten to tell him about it sooner. The skateboarding club in Ben's neighborhood had shut down over the summer. His father had asked his mother if it'd be okay for Ben to join the club that Carter belonged to. His mother, of course, said yes without asking Carter first.

"Mom," Carter said. "It's the club me and my friends belong to. I don't want him there. And I don't want Dad coming there either."

"But you used to like it when he came to your Little League games," she said.

"That was ages ago," Carter said. "And anyway, I only played baseball because you made me."

"Well, you used to enjoy spending weekends with your dad and Ben," she said.

Ben was born shortly after Carter's mom and dad divorced. His dad didn't marry Ben's mom, but he did meet and marry someone else a few years ago, when his little brother was six or seven. Before that, Carter would spend every other weekend at his dad's. After that, everything had changed.

His dad had inherited a whole new family. His new wife had a daughter and a son, who were older than Carter. Their dad had less time for Carter once he had four kids' soccer games and band concerts to attend. Carter had also felt out of place, being the only Hispanic kid in the middle of a big white family. It had especially annoyed him when his dad would playfully call him *gordito*, and his dad's new family would laugh, thinking his dad was calling him fat. His new step-siblings had always called him "little fatty."

"That was before Dad got married," Carter told his mom. "Before everything changed."

His mom shot him her tired-eyes look, a look she saved for such occasions. A look that said she'd had just about enough of his childishness.

Then the phone rang.

It didn't take long for Carter to guess who was on the other end. He heard Ben's name come up a couple of times, and he could tell by the looks his mom cast his way that she was talking to his dad.

Carter didn't get the full story, but when Ben got home that night, their dad had asked him how things went at the skateboarding club. He wanted to know if Carter had introduced him to everybody. Carter wasn't sure what Ben had told their dad, but whatever it was, it wasn't good. Carter's mom took away his skating privileges for a week. That meant he wouldn't get any practice time in at the skatepark before next Thursday's skate-off.

The next day at school, his friends all sympathized with him.

"Man, that bites," Sprig said.

"It'll be okay," Chatty said. "You've been skating all summer. Your moves are fresh."

But Carter wasn't so sure of that. When Sprig or Chatty were on, they could match him trick for trick. A couple of the seventh graders were solid. Then there was Ben. Carter saw how fluid he was on the halfpipe. He had skills. He could complicate things for Carter.

Back when he was in sixth grade, Carter had made it to just one traveling event. He remembered how angry the older kids got. They didn't feel he had earned the right to represent the team. To them, putting in the time was just as important as being the better skater. But now, he'd earned that right. He had put in the time, and he had the skills. This was supposed to be his year.

Ben could be a threat to Carter's status — and his crew's status — on the skate club. He shared this worry with his friends.

"Aw, don't worry about him," Sprig said.

"Yeah, he won't be a problem," Chatty added.

The next week was hard on Carter. Sprig and Chatty would talk about hitting the skatepark after school to get in some extra skate time. Carter even had to miss Monday's practice, so he couldn't see how his competition was stacking up.

His friends had filled him in later. Ben had showed up with his dad — *their* dad. The dad Carter hardly ever saw. Sprig and Chatty wouldn't talk about the tricks Ben did, even though it was clear that Chatty really wanted to. But by the looks in their eyes, they were impressed. And they were worried.

After Carter rode the bus home from school, his mother at least allowed him some practice time at home before it was time to eat dinner. He had built a three-foot quarterpipe. It was a beast and as heavy as a house, with a two-foot-wide deck on the backside. But Carter was determined. He managed to drag it out of the garage by himself and into the driveway.

He started simple — he skated up the ramp, held a nosestall, and then rolled to fakie. When he hit the ramp the next time, he did a rock and roll, and came back at the ramp with a frontside ollie. He liked the sound of his wheels slapping the wooden ramp when he landed the trick, but after just a couple of them, his mother poked her head out the door.

"*¡No hagas tanto ruido!*" she scolded him as she looked around to see if the noise had disturbed any of their neighbors.

Next up, an ollie blunt. Carter rolled quickly up the ramp and caught the coping between his back truck and tail. He did an indy grab as he popped back and rolled fakie down the ramp.

By the time his mother called him to come in for dinner, Carter was completely exhausted, and his T-shirt was soaked through with sweat. But it was worth it. He at least felt like he'd be ready to skate for a spot on the traveling squad on Thursday.

On Thursday, Sprig and Chatty joined him for lunch, as usual. Carter could tell something was up with them. They acted as if they had something to hide. He just couldn't figure out what it was. Yet he knew if he gave Chatty enough time, he would probably spill the beans.

"So what's up?" Carter asked. "How's the competition looking for the skate-off?"

"I don't think we have much to worry about," Sprig said.

"At least we won't be having any trouble with your little bro," Chatty said between mouthfuls of tater tots.

"What's that supposed to mean?" Carter asked.

"Um . . . we didn't do any—" Chatty stammered.

"Chatty, shut up," Sprig cut him off.

"Guys, if I get another call from my dad about Ben, my mom will just take my board away," Carter warned his friends. "I won't be part of the club anymore."

His friends quickly changed the subject and turned the discussion to the runs they were planning later that day. Chatty focused on the halfpipe, and Sprig the street course. They each had some of their favorite tricks lined up. If Carter had his way, he would school them both. This was supposed to be his year.

* * *

After school, Carter grabbed his gear from his mom's car.

"Be nice to Ben," she yelled as he ran off with his board tucked under one arm and his backpack slung over his shoulder.

He was in a hurry to get to the skatepark. Sure, he'd been practicing his street moves all week, but he hadn't been on a ramp bigger than his homemade quarterpipe. He was worried

that he might be a little rusty. So today, there wasn't time for any tricks on his way to the skatepark. He just skated as fast as he could, hoping to get there early enough to get in a little work on Big Vert.

Luck wasn't on his side. When he arrived at the skatepark, a couple of the younger club members were out on the street course, but the majority of the skaters were inside. And they were almost all wanting to get a crack at Big Vert. Carter had to settle for Little Vert. He managed to do a few 180s and handplants, but he felt rushed and shaky landing some of his tricks.

At four o'clock, Rubin called a stop to their warm-ups. Everyone came inside and gathered around him.

"Okay, time to get things rolling," Rubin said. "We'll start out on the street course. Since this our first skate-off of the year, the order will be determined by age, youngest to oldest. Next time, though, the order goes by how well everyone skated at the last skate-off, worst to first. Got it?"

Rubin looked around as everyone nodded.

"Then let's head on out."

Outside, a couple of members from the senior club waited for them. The older skaters would be scoring everyone's runs.

For their runs, each skater was given two minutes to hit as many tricks as they could. Scoring was based partially on landing tricks, but also on style. And playing it safe wasn't encouraged. Skaters would score points for landing simple tricks, but they'd also score style points for failed attempts at more difficult tricks. So if they didn't push their limits, they'd lose out on style points.

The first couple of sixth graders ran through the typical nosestalls, ollies, and kickflips. They were nervous and shaky.

For most of them, this was something new. They had never been put on the spot in front of more experienced skaters like this, actually competing versus just showing off for their friends.

One kid earned a few raspberries when he missed a feeble frontside, and another took a tumble when she caught her front wheels on the coping as she tried to roll back to fakie on a blunt stall.

Carter and his crew basically stood off to the side and chatted as the sixth graders did their runs. They acted nonchalant, pretending not to pay attention to what the younger skaters were doing, as if it didn't matter to them. It was all a head game. Out of the corner of their eyes, they could see the younger skaters casting nervous glances in their direction. They were wondering what they'd have to do to impress the eighth graders.

Carter and his friends had learned this trick over the past two years. The older skaters had pulled it on them. And it worked. It messed with their heads and rattled their confidence. At least until they started hitting tricks that caused the older skaters to take notice. Once the younger

skaters did something to make the older members of the club pay attention, the spell was broken.

When Ben took to the course, Carter couldn't help but drop the act a little. He wanted to see what his half brother could do. He'd seen him on the halfpipe, and Ben was impressive, but the street course was a different beast. Curiosity got the best of Carter.

Ben dropped in with a caveman. With that move, it didn't look like he was suffering from the mind game that the older kids were playing. Ben clearly meant business. And he skated aggressively from trick to trick. He kickflipped up to a backside 5-0 across one of the platforms. Not only did that get the attention of the seventh graders, but Carter heard Chatty whisper to Sprig. "Wow. He made that look really easy."

"Just wait," Sprig whispered back.

Then Ben skated up to one of the rails. It looked as if he was ollieing up for a nosegrind, but something went wrong. As the nose of his board and the weight of his body came down on the rail, the deck seemed to give way, and Ben tumbled over the bar, landing hard on the concrete.

There were sympathetic groans from everyone gathered around the course. They had all taken similar spills. They all knew what hitting pavement felt like.

Ben got up and walked over to his board. He looked a little shaken. He had some nasty scrapes across one of his forearms and a fresh scuff on his elbow pad. There was even some blood trickling down to his fingers.

Before he could jump back on his board and attempt to finish the run, Rubin called over to him.

"You all right?" he asked Ben.

Ben nodded, but it was more of an instinctual nod. Almost everyone said they were okay after taking a spill — whether they were or not. They wanted to prove they could tough it out in front of everybody else. But Carter could see it in Ben's eyes that he was done for this run. He was hurting.

CARTER'S RUN

Carter had seen it happen to a lot of inexperienced skaters during their first competitions. A fall that they might shake off while practicing would completely throw them off during a competition. And if they kept skating, it could lead to a worse fall — and worse injuries.

Almost without thinking, Carter walked away from his friends and joined Rubin as he chatted with Ben. Thankfully, Rubin also recognized that Ben was done.

"Go inside and get checked out," Rubin told Ben. "If all's okay, and you're up for it, join us at the halfpipe later. And Carter, get off the course!"

Ben picked up his board and brushed by Carter without saying a word. He strode purposefully toward the entrance of the skatepark. Ben acted as if he were embarrassed about what had happened. But Carter could tell by everyone's reaction that he had nothing to worry about. No one was smiling or mocking his fall.

Well, no one except Carter's friends. When he walked back over to them, Sprig and Chatty were whispering something and trying to smother giggles.

"Man, what's wrong with you?" Carter asked. "He could have been hurt."

"Why do you care?" Sprig asked.

"Yeah, you don't even like your brother," Chatty added.

They continued to chuckle to themselves. Their snickering was drawing the attention of some of the younger skaters, and Carter could tell it was weighing on their nerves. The seventh graders did only slightly better than the sixth graders.

Then it was the eighth graders' turn. Chatty went first. His run was okay, but Carter could tell he was holding back. He would do a straight ollie as he went up for his grinds instead of adding a kickflip, and whenever he attempted a spin he'd opt for a 180 instead of a 360. He wasn't pushing it. Carter figured he was saving himself for Big Vert.

Once his score was tallied, Chatty was in second place, after one of the seventh graders. That meant that if both Carter and Sprig had solid runs, they would knock him off.

When Carter began his run, he instinctively performed a caveman off a ledge. At first, he wasn't exactly sure why he did that particular trick. It was a fairly simple trick, holding the board out in front of him and jumping on while it was still in the air. Maybe it was a way of honoring his brother. He wondered how Ben was doing. Then Carter remembered why this trick was so significant, why Ben probably started his run with it. Why he felt like he had to start off with it, too. The caveman was the first trick he had taught his little brother.

Carter skated up to one of the quarterpipes. Near the top of the vert, he did a kickflip and rolled fakie down the ramp. Then he hit a switch 180 ollie back to regular. He wanted to show off some of the things he'd been working on at home, so he mostly hit the spines and ramps. He pulled off an ollie blunt and then went for an ollie, making sure his wheels

slapped the ramp hard. He could just hear his mother yelling, "*¡No hagas tanto ruido!*" at the sound that trick made. Hit fit in a 5-0 grind across one of the rails. Then he ended with a pressure flip, an old-school trick that most of the younger kids probably hadn't even seen before. He hoped it left an impression on them. Maybe this was going to be his year after all.

HALFPIPE

His run put him in first place. Then Sprig was up. His friend must have been feeling a bit cocky, because from a frontside feeble to a blunt stall, he hit every trick he had seen one of the younger kids miss earlier. Carter got a chuckle out of that, until Sprig went up for a nose grind on the very same rail that Ben tumbled over earlier.

Chatty was snickering off to the side, and Carter started to feel like something was up with his friends. They had a secret that they weren't telling him.

Sprig finished in second place, so that meant Carter and Sprig would be traveling for sure. Now it was off to the halfpipe. Same basic rules for this event.

The sixth graders, already a bit rattled, didn't fare so well. They kept it simple with some 180s and grabs.

Carter was surprised that Rubin skipped right over Ben's turn. He actually hadn't seen his little brother since he'd stomped off the street course. Carter looked around for Ben as the seventh graders did their runs. Ben was hanging back by the entrance. One hand was bandaged up, and he was holding his board by the tail with his other hand. Carter walked over to him.

"What's up?" Carter asked. "How come you weren't out there on the halfpipe."

"I'm just waiting for Dad to pick me up," Ben said. "Why do you care?"

Carter didn't know how to respond to that. He had never made his brother feel very welcome here, and Ben must be feeling somewhat bitter after that tough fall. So Carter reached over and grabbed his brother's board.

"Something wrong with your deck?" Carter asked.

He saw that the nose was beat up and splintered. It looked like an old and well used board. But now it was basically ruined.

"Rubin has a couple of spare boards in the back if you want . . ." Carter's voiced trailed off as he examined Ben's board further. The skull on the bottom of the deck was faded and scratched, but it looked familiar. He swore that this was the old Powell board he had asked his dad for ages ago. That was back when he wanted all his skater gear and clothing to have skulls on them. That was the cool thing then.

"Where'd you get this?" Carter asked Ben.

"You left it at Dad's place," Ben reminded him. "Remember, you kept it there because your mom didn't want you skating. She kept signing you up for Little League, even though you hated it."

"You remember that?" Carter asked.

"Just like I remember Dad dragging me to all your games," Ben said. "They were painful."

"Yeah, I wasn't any good," Carter said. "But why do you have this board?"

"When you stopped coming around, Dad gave it to me," Ben said. "I remembered some of the tricks you'd showed me —"

"The caveman?" Carter interrupted.

"So you caught that?" Ben said, smiling for the first time during their conversation.

"Yeah, I did," Carter said. "Nice move."

Carter thought back on his visits with his dad and Ben, when it had been just the three of them. Ben had always looked up to Carter, his big brother. He'd tagged along when their dad came to Carter's baseball games and birthday parties. He had watched, amazed, as Carter had landed his first ollie and kickflip. Then he had begged Carter to teach him some tricks.

"Well, good to see it's being put to use," Carter said with a smile. "I had totally forgotten about this deck."

And that's when it hit Carter. When his dad married, it wasn't so much that he lost his dad to another family, but that he lost a little brother. Suddenly Ben had a new, bigger brother to look up to. And he saw this new older brother a lot more often. Carter felt like he had been knocked down the pecking order.

"Ya know," Ben said. "I'm not so sure about joining this club. I cut out of school early on Mondays and Thursdays just to get here on time. And Dad's annoyed that he has to drive me all the way across town when there's a skate club not far from us."

"Wait a second," Carter broke in. "My mom said that the club near you closed down."

"Nah, it's not closed," Ben said. "I just don't like it there. The kids are all about who's the best at this trick or who can do that trick versus just carving it up and having some fun. I wasn't learning anything, not like when I used to watch you."

"That was ages ago," Carter said.

"Yeah, but it was fun," Ben said. "I thought it'd be fun here, skating with you again."

Carter suddenly felt like the worst brother ever. This whole time, he had been thinking his little brother was here to cut in on his turf, to show him up, when this was supposed to be his year to shine. But he'd had Ben all wrong. He just wanted a big brother he could look up to, to impress, to skate with. A brother who could be proud of him.

"Come on, bro," Carter said. "I've seen you skate. You don't need to learn much from me."

"I'm not so sure about that," Ben said. "You seem to have this natural connection with your board. Your tricks, like that pressure flip, seem effortless. Where'd you dig that one up anyway?"

"You saw that?" Carter asked.

"Yeah, I snuck back out quick after getting doctored up," Ben said, raising his bandaged arm up.

"Well, I was grounded from the skatepark," Carter said. "So between practice sessions on my own quarterpipe, I was stuck at home watching old videos of the Birdman. That was a personal fave of his."

Carter was surprised how easy it was talking to his little brother. Unlike with his friends, he didn't feel like he needed to keep up a "cool" front all the time. With Ben, he could get down to the nuts and bolts of moves and not focus so much on the final result of whether or not he landed the trick.

"Carter! Yo, Carter," Rubin called for him. "You're up."

"You don't want to miss your run," Ben said.

"Yeah, okay," Carter said. He turned from his little brother and ran over to Big Vert.

Before climbing up to the deck, Carter stopped to chat with Rubin.

"What about Ben?" he asked.

"He passed on his run," Rubin said. "Said he was feeling a little woozy after that spill."

"What if he's feeling better now?" Carter asked. "You've seen him skate. Shouldn't we give him a shot for the team's sake?"

"Yeah, yeah, whatever," Rubin muttered. "Just do your run. I'd like to get out of here sometime before the New Year."

Not surprisingly, Carter's run didn't amount to much. He was feeling rusty after nearly a week away from the halfpipe. His inverts and stalls were solid. He even tested out a variation of an ollie pop 180. But when he tried hitting a 360 backside with a nose grab, he over spun and ended up sliding down the ramp on his back.

He finished in third place, with Chatty in first and some seventh grader in second. But those positions weren't final until Sprig skated and Ben took his crack, if he was even going to skate.

While Sprig was skating, Carter ran over to his little brother. He handed Ben his board.

"What exactly do you want me to do with this?" Ben asked.

"Rubin said if you're up for it, you can still do your run," Carter said. "If you liked my old board so much, maybe this one will do for now."

Ben gave him a look like he wasn't sure he could trust Carter.

"You sure?" he asked.

All Carter had to do was nod.

Ben ran up to Rubin with Carter's board in hand. They had a quick chat, and then Ben was climbing up onto the platform. As he was going up, Sprig was coming down. His friend gave his little brother a dirty look, but Ben ignored it. He was too focused on the task at hand.

Ben dropped in and skated up the other side of the ramp. He seemed a little shaky at first, probably still recovering from his earlier spill. He did a couple of frontside 180s. Then he went in for a nosegrind across the coping, and that was all he needed. He raced up the other side of the ramp for a ho-ho, the board resting on his feet while he did a handstand on the coping. Then he grabbed his deck and dropped down, quickly racing up the other end of the ramp for an ollie with a nose grab. Midair, he looked in Carter's direction and pointed at him.

As Ben pulled off that trick, Sprig and Chatty turned to Carter.

"Dude, what'd you do?" Chatty asked.

"You're ruining our plan," Sprig said.

"What are you guys talking about?" Carter asked, but then he rethought it. "Let's just watch the rest of his run."

Carter turned back in time to see Ben go for a Madonna by shooting up the frontside, grabbing the nose while taking his front foot and extending it downward and quickly putting it back on the board before slapping the tail on the coping and rolling back into the ramp.

He was all smiles as he climbed down from the top of Big Vert.

While his scores were being tallied, Carter turned back to his friends. "Now what were you talking about before?" "We had this plan, you see," Chatty began.

"Chatty, come on, don't tell him," Sprig said.

"But he ruined it, so he's gotta know," Chatty said. "Anyway, Ben left his board in the lockers Monday. Sprig and I figured if we messed with it a bit, we could make sure he didn't show any of us up."

"Serious?" Carter said. "You broke into his locker? That's low."

Sure, at first he hadn't wanted Ben to succeed here either. But sabotage had never crossed his mind. He had planned to out-skate him, just as he had planned to out-skate everyone else.

"He could've been hurt," Carter said, turning from his friends.

He paused just long enough at the door to hear that Ben took third, behind Chatty and a seventh grader. He had bumped his big brother out of a spot on the halfpipe. It was bittersweet. Carter had missed a chance to double up on events, but his little brother would be traveling with him. They would both be representing their skate club this Saturday.

The next day at school was a rough one for Carter. He was still upset by what his friends had pulled, and they ended up arguing over lunch.

"What? You want us to 'fess up?" Sprig said, sounding baffled.

"Rubin would kick us out of the club," Chatty added.

"No, no, I don't care about telling him," Carter tried explaining. "Ben. Tell Ben. Apologize and make him feel welcome at the club. He's my little bro."

"So he's your 'bro' now?" Spring said, getting angry.

"Ya know, this isn't just about Ben, either," Carter said. "It's about how we treat all the sixth and seventh graders like dirt to get an edge on them. That's how it's always been, but what you did to Ben just took it too far."

The conversation didn't end well as they all stormed off in their separate directions. With his brother and those two in a car tomorrow, things were going to get tense. He hoped it wouldn't affect their performances at the competition.

But that wasn't the worst of it. After school, Carter ran out to his mother's car to wait for his mom. When she came outside, he got his board and gear from the trunk. Then he headed to the skatepark. On his way, he ran through his usual tricks — some ollies and kickflips.

Carter was enjoying listening to his wheels hum along on the pavement when he decided to a try a trick he hadn't hit in a while, a 360 pop shuvit. He ollied up, spun the board with his back foot, and came down with both feet on the deck. He was about to do a celebratory fist pump when disaster struck. Carter heard a loud crack. Then his board lurched sideways under his feet, sending him hard to the ground.

"Umpf!" he gasped as he hit concrete.

Carter lay there on his back for several long moments as the pain from his fall slowly faded to numbness. Then Carter

grunted and rolled over. He saw his board off in the grass. When he picked it up, he was horrified. One of the trucks had cracked, and half of it still lay on the ground at his feet.

Picking up the broken piece of his skateboard, Carter was overwhelmed by the concerns racing through his mind. Would he even be able to compete on Saturday? Would Ben? They both had busted boards now. And while he knew his friends were trying to help him out, they had crossed the line. How could they stoop so low? Did he say something that had encouraged them?

As Carter cringed in pain, one last thought crossed his mind: his fall was nothing compared to his little brother's. Then something inside snapped. He'd had enough. He was angry — beyond angry. Carrying his busted-up board, Carter ran to the skatepark. He was pretty sure that Sprig and Chatty would be there. They'd want to get in a little practice before the competition tomorrow.

When the park was in sight, he saw Sprig on the street course. He was working the rails. Carter walked straight up to him and pushed him off his board midtrick.

"What the —" Sprig cursed as he lay the ground.

He tried to get back up, but Carter just pushed him back down.

"How's it feel, huh?" Carter shouted. "Messing with Ben's board. I didn't ask you to do that!"

"We didn't do it for you," Spring said, not able to meet Carter's eyes. "Between you and Ben, Chatty and I were worried we'd never get to compete. This is supposed to be our year. And since you didn't seem to like Ben much, we just thought . . ."

Sprig rose up to his elbows

"Look, we know we messed up," Sprig said. "We'll come clean with Ben when we see him next."

"Serious?" Carter asked, not sure he could trust his friend anymore.

"Listen, bro, Chatty and I felt pretty bad after our argument today," Sprig explained. "So we decided to skate over here with some of the young guns."

Carter looked around him. A crowd had gathered. He recognized some of the kids from the club. One was the seventh grader who would be competing on the street course with them tomorrow. The crowd nodded, verifying Sprig's story.

Carter reached down and helped his friend up. He knew he had let his anger get the best of him, and he felt bad about it.

"I'm sorry, Carter. We should never mess with another skater's gear," Sprig said, looking down at the board in Carter's hand. "Hey, what happened to that?"

"Broke a truck doing a pop shuvit on the way over," Carter said.

"Do you have a spare deck?" Sprig asked.

"I don't know," Carter sighed. "I might be able to piece something together."

Just then Carter's mom's car rolled up into the parking lot.

"Carter, come on," his mother called to him. "I forgot to tell you we're going to have company tonight."

On the way home, she wouldn't tell him who was coming over, but Carter recognized the car parked out in front of the house. It was his dad's. He and Ben got out as they pulled into the driveway.

"Mom, how could you forget to tell me they were coming over?" Carter said.

"*Lo siento,*" was all his mother said as she ran into the house, leaving Carter alone with Ben and their dad.

Ben ran up to him, excited.

"Dad's taking me to get a new skateboard," he said. "He figures I can finally get something that isn't a hand-me-down."

"Well, good for you," Carter replied. He knew he was being a jerk, but he was tired of always feeling like he got the short end of the stick.

Ben was taken aback. It wasn't the response he had expected from his brother, not after how they had connected yesterday. Carter saw the hurt in Ben's eyes and immediately felt bad.

"I'm sorry, it's just —" Carter tried to explain by telling Ben about his fall and broken board, but he was interrupted by their dad.

"What happened there?" he asked, pointing to the broken truck on Carter's board.

"Whoa," Ben said. "You must have taken a spill?"

"Yeah, it busted as I was landing a shuvit," Carter said.

"You okay, son?" his dad asked.

Carter felt like he was on the verge of crying. He was having a rough day with his friends, his deck was messed, and now one of the people he least wanted to talk to was asking him about it all.

All Carter could do was nod.

"Well, hey, *gordito*, let me talk to your mom," his dad said, putting his hand on Carter's shoulder. "Maybe I can get both my sons new skateboards."

"I'm not a little kid anymore, Dad," Carter said.

Without losing a beat, his dad responded, "Okay, *gordo*, but don't you wanna come with us to pick out a new plank? I know I want you to."

"It's called a deck, Dad," Ben shot back.

The boys just shook their heads.

While their dad went inside to talk to his mother, Carter showed Ben the quarterpipe he had built.

"So this is where you've learned all the moves," Ben said. "It looks pretty solid."

"It weighs a ton, though," Carter added.

They waited a while, not sure what the grown-ups were talking about inside.

"You don't think he's gonna make us get matching skateboards, do you?" Ben asked.

"Knowing Dad, he'd think that's funny," Carter said.

"You still into skulls?" Ben asked.

"No, unicorns," Carter said with a straight face.

"Serious?" Ben asked.

"No, bro, I'm just messing with you," Carter said with a chuckle.

A moment later, they were both cracking up, their peals of laughter echoing through the neighborhood.

Carter and Ben both regularly represent the skate club at traveling events. They're competitive, yet supportive, of one another. But no matter what happens in competition, they always go out for pizza together afterward.

Carter's story has inspired custom skateboard and sticker designs.

L2S Rival

L2S Ramos Hawk Face

L2S Skull Phase

SKATE CLINIC:
CAVEMAN

1. Hold your board by the nose. Use your left hand if you ride regular or your right hand if you ride goofy.

2. Jump off of your obstacle, holding the board under your feet.

3. When your feet connect with the board, let go of it.

4. As you land, be sure to bend your knees. This will help you absorb the impact and stay upright.

SKATE CLINIC:
TERMS

5-0 grind
a move where a skater pops up onto an obstacle, then grinds his or her trucks along it

feeble grind
a move where the skater grinds a rail with the back truck while the front truck hangs over the rail's far side

ho-ho
a move where the skater does a handstand with both hands on the coping while the feet are fully extended and the board rests on top of the feet

indy grab
a grab where the skater places his or her back hand on the toeside of the board

kickflip
a move where the skater pops the skateboard into the air and flicks it with the front foot to make it flip all the way around in the air before landing on the board again

nose grab
a grab where the skater grabs the front of the board with the front hand while the feet are in an ollie position

nosegrind
a move where the skater grinds across the obstacle with only the front truck

ollie
a move where the skater pops the board into the air with his or her feet

pop shuvit
a move where the skater ollies and spins the board 180 degrees before landing on the board again

pressure flip
a flip trick that is popped and flipped with the same foot; pressure flips are done with a scooping movement, rather than popping the board like in an ollie.

rock and roll
a move where the skater places the front truck over the lip of the ramp and then rocks the board slightly before turning 180 degrees and rolling back into the ramp

written by

BLAKE A. HOENA

Blake A. Hoena grew up in central Wisconsin, where he wrote stories about robots conquering the moon and trolls lumbering around the woods behind his parents' house. He now lives in Minnesota and continues to write about fun things like space aliens and superheroes. Blake has written more than fifty chapter books and graphic novels for children.

pencils and colors by

FERNANDO CANO

Fernando Cano is an all-around artist living in Monterrey, Mexico. He currently works as a concept artist for a video game company, CGbot. Having published with Marvel, DC, Pathfinder, and IDW, he spends his free time playing video games, singing, writing, and above all, drawing!

inks by

JOE AZPEYTIA

Joe Azpeytia currently lives in Mexico and works as a freelance graphic designer for music bands and international companies. Currently an illustration artist at The Door on the Wall studio, he enjoys playing drums, playing video games, and drawing.